HERCULES
CHAMPION OF THE WORLD

HERCULES
CHAMPION OF THE WORLD

STORY BY
NIGEL GRAY

ILLUSTRATIONS BY
HEATH McKENZIE

**WALKER
BOOKS**

First published in Great Britain 2013 by Walker Books Ltd
87 Vauxhall Walk, London SE11 5HJ

10 9 8 7 6 5 4 3 2 1

Text © 2012 Nigel Gray
Illustrations © 2012 Heath McKenzie

The right of Nigel Gray and Heath McKenzie to be identified as author and illustrator respectively of this work has been asserted by them in accordance with the Copyright, Designs and Patents Act 1988

This book has been typeset in Univers.

Printed and bound in Great Britain by Clays Ltd, St Ives plc

British Library Cataloguing in Publication Data:
a catalogue record for this book is available from
the British Library

ISBN 978-1-4063-4783-8

www.walker.co.uk

For my Kalamunda cronies,
Greg, Keith and Ken. NG

For Em, as we prepare to embark on
our own task of Herculean proportions! HM

HERCULES'S JOURNEYS THROUGHOUT GREECE

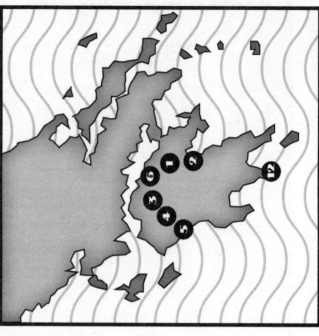

1. Nemea (The Lion of Doom)
2. Lerna (The Seven-headed Hydra)
3. Ceryneia (The Golden Hind)
4. Erymanthus (The Wild Boar)
5. Elis (The Stables of King Augeas)
6. Stymphalos (Birds of the Stymphalian Marsh)
7. Crete (The White Bull)
8. Thrace (The Hungry Horses of King Diomedes)
9. Cappadocia (Molly Muscles and the Amazon belt)
10. Tartessus (King Gerry's Cattle)
11. The Garden of the Hesperides (The Golden Apples)
12. The Underworld (The Hound of Hell, Cerberus)

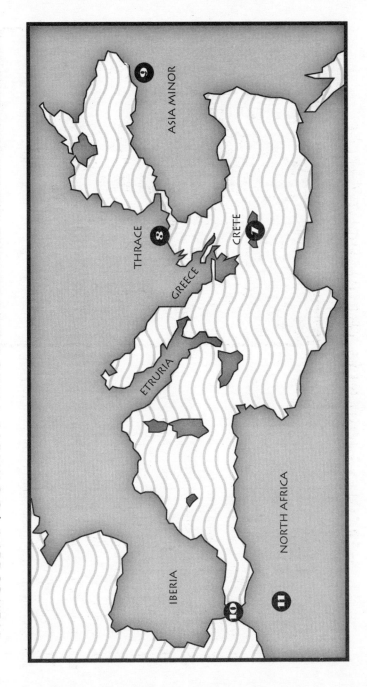

CHAPTER ONE
THE WICKED STEPMOTHER

When Hercules[1] was a baby, he was one of those big, bouncing, rubbery, blubbery ones. He had a grip like a pair of boltcutters even then. He had a wicked stepmother[2] too, who put two snakes into his cot one night. But before the snakes could even poke their forked tongues out at him, Hercules strangled them both.

[1] Hercules is the Roman name for a legendary Greek hero called Heracles.

[2] His wicked stepmother was a goddess called Hera.

11

Hercules was one of those kids who is best at everything. (Don't you hate them?) He had the biggest muscles. He was the best looking. He was the best shot with a bow and arrow. He was the best at clubbing anything that moved. He was the best swordsman. He was the best charioteer.[3] He was the best horserider. He was the best wrestler. He was the best boxer. He was the best singer. He was the best at playing the lyre.[4]

When Hercules grew up he married a woman called Megara. Hercules and Meg had three sons and they were all very happy. But his wicked

[3] A charioteer was a person who drove a chariot. A chariot was a two-wheeled, horse-drawn vehicle used in warfare and racing.

[4] A lyre is an instrument like a guitar without a neck. A lyrebird, though, is not a bird that plays the lyre. Nor, indeed, is it a bird without a neck.

stepmother was cruel and jealous. She hated seeing him so cock-a-hoop[5] and decided to do the nastiest, meanest, most horrible thing she could think of – something that would destroy his happiness forever. It's hard to imagine anyone being that mean, but she put a spanner in the works and used her special goddess powers to cause him to have a breakdown (even though he didn't have a car). Hercules, I'm sorry to have to tell you, was driven bananas, which resulted in him doing something unimaginable and terrible. While he was stark-raving bonkers he killed his wife and children. When his fit of madness passed, he couldn't believe what he'd done. He cried for hours. He promised never to do it again. But it was a bit late for that. He decided it might not be a bad idea to make himself scarce[6] before anyone found out.

Hercules was in a state. It was a state he didn't like being in, so he went to another one. In that state, his half-brother Eurystheus was the king.[7] Eury didn't like Hercules one bit. Hercules was better than Eury

5 Cock-a-hoop means strutting about proudly and boastfully, like a rooster.

6 To make yourself scarce means to skedaddle; that is to say, to run away as fast as you can.

7 Eurystheus was the king of Mycenae.

at everything. Eury looked like the back end of a chariot. When he sang, he sounded like a bullfrog with laryngitis.**8** And he couldn't play the lyre to save his life.

Eurystheus told Hercules he wouldn't turn him in if Hercules could complete twelve tasks. Hercules's heart sank. *I suppose*, he thought, *I'll have to chop the firewood, get the shopping, scrub the floors, empty the toilets* (they didn't have flush toilets in those days), *clean out the pigsty* and so on. But he didn't have much choice.

"Okay," he said, "I promise to do any jobs you ask me to do, and to do them to the best of my ability."

"Right," said Eury. "Your first task is to kill the Lion of Nemea."

"Okay," said Hercules. "No worries."

That's the sort of bloke he was. He'd rather kill a lion than clean a toilet.

"Oh, and by the way," said Eury, "you have to skin it and bring back its hide[9] to prove you've killed it."

[9] A hide is not the animal's den as you might imagine – a hide is the skin of an animal.

"No worries," said Hercules. "No probs. No drama."

But what Hercules didn't know was that the Lion of Nemea was no ordinary lion. People called it the Lion of Doom. It was big. Very big. It was strong. Very strong. But that wasn't all. Its hide was so thick and tough that no weapon that had ever been made could pierce it. (This was in the days before they'd invented bazookas.[10])

[10] A bazooka is a modern anti-tank weapon.

So Hercules went away and girded up his loins.[11]

[11] To gird up your loins means to put on a sort of nappy and prepare yourself for what has to be done.

CHAPTER TWO
THE LION OF NEMEA

Hercules set out for the hills where the Lion of Doom hung out. The people of that district were a sorry lot. They were sorry because the lion had eaten lots of their friends and relations.

"No worries," said Hercules to the locals. "Leave it to me. I'll put a stop to Larry's[12] shenanigans.[13]"

Hercules followed the lion's tracks to the cave where it slept. (He was the best

[12] Hercules had a habit of giving nicknames to scary people and creatures. By doing this he made them less scary. This is something you could try for yourself.

[13] Shenanigans is a word I like. It means mischief of one sort or another.

at tracking.) Larry wasn't home. Hercules lurked[14] by the lair (he was the best at lurking).

[14] To lurk means to hang around in hiding when you're up to no good.

After Hercules had lurked for an hour or two, the lion showed up. Larry usually ate out, and he had been out for lunch. He'd had a few sheep for starters, a couple of shepherds for the main course and a sheepdog for dessert. The Lion of Doom was fearsome. And blood dripped from his teeth (he was a messy eater).

Hercules bounded out from behind a rock. He threw his spear with all his strength at the rear end of the Lion of Doom. (He was the best at throwing a spear.) The spear hit Larry in the right buttock, and bounced off.

"What cheek!" the lion said, and looked around

17

to see what had flicked him.

But Hercules was already back behind his rock. He leaped out again and fired his bow and arrow. The arrow hit Larry's left buttock, but that arrow too bounced off. The lion looked around again, and swished his tail angrily. He wasn't used to such impudence.[15]

Hercules drew his sword. Not on a sketchpad, you understand, but out of its scabbard.[16] He rushed out from his hiding place. He screamed a bloodcurdling scream. It was intended to make the enemy's hair stand on end, but the Lion of Nemea didn't turn a hair. His mangy mane just hung down like it always did. Hercules tried to thrust his sword into Larry's soft underparts. The sword bent in half like cardboard. The lion looked around and tried to swat Hercules with its paw, but missed. Hercules ran back to the safety of his rock. This time the lion came after him.

Hercules took up his club. This was the ace up his sleeve. Except that he was wearing a short sheet sort of item that didn't have a sleeve. Even so, this was the ace of clubs. (Hercules had so many weapons he could have done with a golf bag, and a caddy to carry it around.) He climbed on top of his rock.

[15] Impudence means a lack of respect.

[16] A scabbard is a sheath for the blade of a sword or dagger.

Giving his bloodcurdling yell, he sprang off the rock. On landing, he clouted the lion behind the ear with his club. The club broke in half. *I should have brought a spade*, thought Hercules. (You might want to join Hercules's club - but first you'd have to find the two halves.)

From the force of the blow, Larry went a bit wobbly around the knees. Then the lion pounced (in a wobbly sort of way). Hercules ducked and wove (he was the best at ducking and weaving). He jumped onto the lion's back (he was the best at jumping onto lions' backs). Larry leaped like a lord on the tenth day of Christmas.[17] Hercules hung on. He locked his arms around the beast's neck. He tightened his hold, and Larry went down. Hercules kept on squeezing till the lion stopped twitching. Then Hercules squeezed

[17] On the tenth day of Christmas, according to the song, my true love gave to me ten lords a-leaping. But why they were leaping, I haven't a clue.

a bit more for good measure. "If a job's worth doing, it's worth doing well," his wicked stepmum used to say.

Once the lion was dead, the next job was to skin it. Spear, arrow, sword, knife – nothing was able to cut through the hide. There were only eighteen things Hercules could find that were sharp enough: the Lion of Doom's own claws.

Hercules put the lion's head over his own head, like a helmet, and wore the lion's skin like a cloak. Back at court he nearly started a new fashion. Once they'd seen him dressed in his lion, all the young men wanted to wear one. The trouble was that none of them could catch one.

King Eurystheus had been sure that the Lion of Nemea would have Hercules on toast. (No one had told him that lions don't eat toast.) He was not pleased when the Big H turned up wearing the lion skin. In fact he was terrified. So terrified, he jumped into a large urn that stood in his chamber.[18]

"That was a piece of cake," said Hercules to the urn. "What's next?"

18 Chamber: here, does not mean a chamber pot (a pot you pee in). It means a posh private room.

"Cake?" said Eury, all a-tremble inside his urn. "What cake?"

CHAPTER THREE

THE SEVEN-HEADED HYDRA OF LERNA

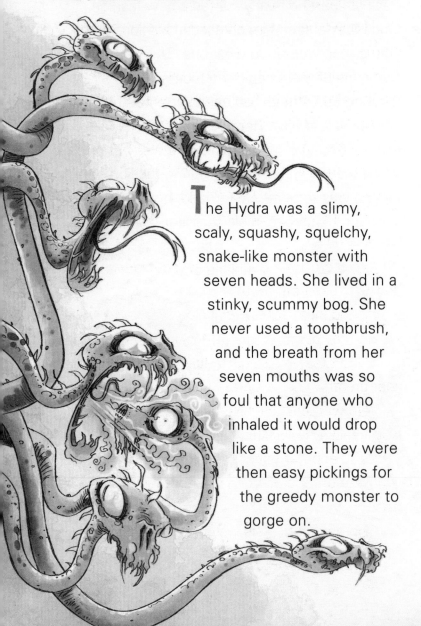

The Hydra was a slimy, scaly, squashy, squelchy, snake-like monster with seven heads. She lived in a stinky, scummy bog. She never used a toothbrush, and the breath from her seven mouths was so foul that anyone who inhaled it would drop like a stone. They were then easy pickings for the greedy monster to gorge on.

"I want you to kill the Hydra of Lerna," King Eurystheus told Hercules. "That'll learn ya. And don't come back unless you do."

"No worries," said Hercules. "No probs. No drama."

Hercules remembered how useful a caddy would have been on his previous task. So he asked his young cousin, Iolaus, to go with him. They didn't have a golf cart, so they loaded the weapons into a chariot and Iolaus drove that. When they reached the bog, they got bogged.

"We'll continue on foot," said Hercules, hopping down.

"Why are you hopping?" asked Iolaus. "Why don't we use both feet?"

"Good idea," said Hercules.

So they did.

"Don't forget," said Iolaus, "you need to hold your breath."

"No worries," said Hercules. (Hercules was the best at holding his breath.)

"And another thing," said Iolaus. "Every time you chop off one of its heads, another grows in its place."

"No problem," said Hercules. "*I'll* chop off Hilda's head—"

23

"Hilda?" said Iolaus.

"Yes, Hilda," said Hercules. "*You* bring a flaming torch and sear[19] the wound. That way, the new head won't be able to grow."

19 To sear means to seal something by burning it with intense heat.

"Good thinking," said Iolaus.

"Oh, one more thing. Its middle head is immortal. Even if you chop the head off, it still lives and breathes out poisonous gas."

"No drama," said Hercules. "I'll think of something."

So, with his lion skin protecting his back, and the lion head protecting his head, Hercules splashed through the bog. Iolaus followed with his

flaming torch, wearing his underpants on his head. (This was the first gas mask.)

The Hydra breathed seven simultaneous[20] blasts of poison gas at them. But Hercules was so good at holding his breath, he could have been a synchronised swimming champion (except that they hadn't invented synchronised swimming yet). So he just sloshed on through the bog. When he was close enough, he swung his sword. He sliced off one of Hilda's heads. It sank into the muck with a plop and a gurgle.

20 Simultaneous means happening at the same time.

Iolaus rushed forwards. The Hydra was so surprised to see him wearing his underpants on his head, it forgot to blast them with bad breath for a few moments. Iolaus seared the bleeding neck, and no new head began to grow. Iolaus turned around, lifted his underpants and took a quick gulp of air.

Hercules chopped off another head. "Easy-peasy," he said.

Iolaus leaped in, did his stuff and leaped out.

In this way they dealt with six of the seven heads.

All of a sudden, a giant crab caught hold of Hercules's ankle. Hercules stomped on the crab. The crab went splat! Hilda chose this moment to attack with her poison breath. But Hercules was too quick. With one mighty slash of his sword, he sliced off the Hydra's middle and final head.

He fished it, muddy and dripping, out of the bog. He ran with it to dry ground. He threw it down and picked up a huge boulder. The head went splat – just like the crab. Only then did Hercules take a big breath. Hilda was as dead as a dodo.[21]

[21] A dodo was a bird, like a giant pigeon with a duck's bill – now extinct.

"It looks like a pancake," Iolaus said.

"I think it's more like a pizza," said Hercules.

When Iolaus bent down to have a closer look

he nearly scorched Hercules's backside with his torch.

"Mind what you're doing with that flaming torch!" said Hercules.

"No need for bad language!" said Iolaus.

Then Hercules had a good idea. The slime that had oozed out of the Hydra's squashed head was exceptionally poisonous, so he dipped all his arrowheads in it. "You never know when you might need a poison arrow in this job," he said.

So Hercules went back to Eury and told him the deed was done.

"You cheated," said the King.

"I did not," said Hercules.

"You had someone to help you," said Eury. "You can't count that one."

"What!" roared Hercules. He held his breath and went red in the face, and looked as if he was about to chop off *Eury's* head.

Eury ran behind one of his handmaidens.[22] "All right, all right," he said hastily. "We'll count it this time – but just this once."

Hercules took a deep breath and grunted. "So what's next?" he asked.

[22] A handmaiden was a female servant who was always on hand.

CHAPTER FOUR

THE GOLDEN HIND

The best hunter in the land, until Hercules came along, was Artemis, who was the goddess of hunting, who usually hung out in the forests of Ceryneia. Artemis had special powers, but even so, she had been unable to catch a magnificent hind that people called Goldy Horn. This hind was rather extraordinary in that it had solid gold antlers.[23] Nevertheless,

23 It's not usual for a female deer to have antlers, but then again it's not usual for a deer's antlers to be solid gold. Hind, incidentally, which means "female deer", is derived from a ancient word meaning "without horns". Work that out!

Artemis, being a goddess, thought of Goldy as belonging to her, and in the end she decided that if *she* couldn't catch the hind, she'd make sure no one else did. She vowed[24] to kill anyone who spilled a drop of her deer's blood.

[24] To vow is to promise.

King Eurystheus came up with a cunning plan. He would send Hercules to catch this deer. If Hercules failed to catch it, he wouldn't be allowed back into Eury's kingdom. If he did catch it, he would catch it from Artemis. As far as Hercules was concerned, it would be a no-win situation.

Hercules couldn't take his caddy Iolaus this time, so he just took his bow and some non-poisonous arrows. It wasn't difficult to find Goldy's tracks, but as soon as she saw him she showed him a clean pair of heels [25] (she'd just come out of the bath). He was soon trailing her up hill and down dale. He followed the pesky critter [26] through marsh and forest. He stalked her (he was the best at stalking) for a year and a day without ever getting within shooting range.

[25] Actually, to show a clean pair of heels means to scarper so fast that the pursuer can't catch up.

[26] Pesky critter is Wild West slang for a troublesome creature.

Hercules was always too far behind the behind of the hind because she was so fleet of foot. (This does not mean that she wore boats on her feet.) Goldy was so fleet[27] of foot that she could outrun and out-jump even the Big H himself.

The deer also had a good nose.[28] And after a year of running up hill and down dale in a thick lion skin, without having a bath, Hercules was what you might call "on the nose", so the deer (dear thing) always knew when he was coming.

However, Hercules hounded Goldy for so long that she finally began to tire. (Hercules, though, was the best at not getting tired.) The hind stopped for a

[27] Fleet means quick and nimble, like Jack when he jumped over the candlestick.

[28] Though not a red one like her distant cousin, Rudolph.

drink on the bank of a river. She smelled Hercules hot on her heels yet again.

Who is that man? thought the deer. Goldy feared she couldn't stagger another step.

Hercules, wearing his lion outfit, crept closer. He was trying to pretend he was a lion so that the deer wouldn't be afraid. (Hercules was not the brightest star in the galaxy!) Goldy stood with her two front feet together. Deer don't usually stand with their feet together or they fall over. Anyway, it was lucky for Hercules that she did. He fired one arrow. The arrow pierced between the bone and sinew of both feet and nailed the hind's two legs together (not the hind legs, you understand, but the hind's legs). Goldy could run no more.

Hercules threw down his bow and the rest of his arrows. *I won't need them any more*, he thought. He lifted the trembling hind and hoisted it onto his shoulders.

He was now wearing a dead lion *and* a live deer. It was a hot day. It was a long journey over stony ground. He was running with sweat. So he slowed down to a jog. *This must be as bad as it gets*, he thought. Then it got worse.

His way was blocked by the angry Artemis. She was aiming an arrow at his heart. "How dare you interfere with my hind!" she said.

"I never touched your behind," protested Hercules.

"Not my behind, my – oh, never mind. I have vowed to kill anyone who sheds the blood of my deer," she said.

"I didn't shed the blood of your deer," said Hercules. "Look for yourself."

The arrow had passed between the tendon and the bone. No blood had been spilled.

"Very clever," sneered Artemis. "A smart alec, eh?"

"I'm smart, all right," said the Big H. "But I'm not Alec. I'm Hercules."

"I don't care if you're the man in the moon," said Artemis. "You must want to die."

"No," said Hercules. "I don't. Honest."

"Say, 'cross my heart and hope to die'," said Artemis.

"Cross my heart and hope to die," said Hercules.

"There you are," said Artemis. "I knew you wanted to die."

"No, no," said Hercules. "It was a slip of the tongue. I don't want to die."

"Then why are you stealing my deer?"

"I'm not stealing it," said Hercules. "I'm only borrowing it. I just have to show it to King Eury, and then I'll put it back where I found it."

"And pull the arrow out?" asked Artemis.

"Yes," said Hercules.

"And put a plaster on the wound?" asked Artemis.

"Yes," said Hercules.

"Promise?" said Artemis.

"Promise," said Hercules.

"Say, 'cross my heart and hope to die'," said Artemis.

"Cross my heart and hope to die," said Hercules.

"Got you again," said Artemis. "I thought you said you were smart."

Their banter continued for awhile. Hercules was very handsome. He had a great deal of charm. He was so charming that Artemis gave him permission to show the deer to Eury, and then bring it back. She was hoping to see him again.

When Hercules arrived at the palace, King Eurystheus looked out of the open window and saw him with the magnificent hind on his shoulders.

"Okay, I caught it," Hercules called. "I'll take it back now."

But greedy Eury had seen the sunlight glinting on the golden antlers. "No you won't," he said. "I'm going to keep it."

Eury rushed out of the palace, rubbing his hands together. Hercules thought of several things he would like to say to Eury, but he bit his tongue.

"Ouch!" he said. "That hurt." Then he added, "Here you are then." He set the hind gently on the ground and pulled out the arrow that had pinned its feet together.

Goldy instantly legged it back home. She was still fast, even though she had a limp. Eury went limp. "You great nitwit!" he shouted. "Quick! Catch it!"

"You've got to be joking," said Hercules. "You catch it."

"Right," spluttered Eury. "I'll get you for this. I've got another job for you. And believe me, you won't like this one."

"I believe you," said Hercules.

CHAPTER FIVE

THE WILD BOAR OF ERYMANTHUS

News reached the palace of a terrible boar[29] in Erymanthus. You've probably met a terrible bore – but this one was in a class of its own. (Although it wasn't in a class - it had never been to school.) This was a barbarous, brutal, bellicose[30] boar that was not only slaughtering livestock and destroying crops, but feasting on farmers and their families, and even snacking on grannies. The people who lived around the area were bored to death. Hercules's next task was to capture this boar and bring it back alive.

[29] A boar is a grown-up, wild, male pig.

[30] Bellicose means aggressive and always looking for a fight.

"No worries," said Hercules. "No probs. No drama."

That's what you think, thought Eury.

Hercules didn't know who he might bump into on the journey, so he took his sword, his bow with a few poison arrows and his club. He also coiled some rope around his waist. He had worked out a very crafty plan. His plan was to whack the boar over the head and tie it up.

It was a long trek to Erymanthus. The boar, which Hercules decided to call "Piglet", lived high up in the mountains above the snowline, so it was easy enough for Hercules to find its tracks. These led to where Piglet was having his afternoon nap in the shelter of some bushes. Hercules crept up behind him, and his lion skin caught on a dead branch. The branch snapped, making a loud crack. Piglet was having a bad dream. In the dream, someone had invented a gun.

(Bad news for life on Earth!) The boar, normally afraid of neither man nor beast, was startled out of his sleep. Thinking that a hunter was shooting at him with the dream gun, ignoring the wisdom of ages, and sages,[31] he leaped before he looked,[32] and plunged into a deep snowdrift.

31 A sage is a wise man.

32 It is always best to look before you leap.

Hercules bore down on the boar. The boar snorted and slavered (boars are very good at that sort of thing), but it was floundering in deep snow. (I don't know if a flounder[33] can flounder, but a boar definitely can.) Piglet couldn't run away, or even turn

33 A flounder is a flat fish, which is also called a fluke. If you caught one it would probably be a fluke.

around to fight. After a brief wrestle, our hero managed to tie up the wild boar. (You'd be wild too if someone you didn't know rolled you in the snow and tied you up!) Then he heaved Piglet onto his shoulders and set off for Eury's palace.

Hercules bore the boar over hill and vale. By the time he got home, he was bent double under the weight of his burden. When he walked into King Eury's chamber, with Piglet still snorting with rage, Eury thought some huge beast was coming to get him. He screamed in terror, despite having a mouthful of moussaka,[34] and jumped into his urn.

34 Moussaka is something that people eat in Greece (though not in grease). It is made up of lamb, eggplants and tomatoes, with cheese on top. Yummo!

"That was boring," said Hercules. "What's next?"

Eury peeped over the rim of the urn. He saw a monster with three heads. Three pairs of eyes stared at him. He ducked back down in the urn.

"What are you doing in there?" asked Hercules.

Eury peeped out again. "Oh, it's you," he said. He saw the face of Hercules. On his head was the face of the lion. On top of the lion was the outraged boar, still slavering in its fury.

"Here's the boar you wanted," said Hercules.

"Get that thing out of here!" said Eury. He was so frightened that his voice came out in a squeak.[35]

"Where shall I put it?" asked Hercules.

[35] You should never squeak with your mouth full.

"I don't care where you put it!" said Eury from inside the urn. "Just kill it."

"Will that count as my fifth task?" asked Hercules.

"No," snapped Eury. "It's still part of the fourth one."

So, grumbling, Hercules went back outside. First he had to carry out the boar, and then he had to carry out the order. And Eury refused to come out of the urn until he was assured that the creature had indeed been killed.

CHAPTER SIX

CLEANING THE STABLES

King Augeas ruled
a country called Elis.
This king was hideously
ugly, so Big H called him
Gorgeous Augeas. He
owned more cattle and
sheep than anyone else
on Earth. He didn't even
know how many cows
and sheep he had. They
wouldn't stand still long
enough for him to count
them. However, he *had* counted his bulls. There
were three hundred black bulls, two hundred
brown bulls and a dozen white bulls.

All these animals were kept in a row of barns. The barns hadn't been cleaned out for thirty years. Imagine that! The poor creatures were wallowing around in stinky poo up to their oxters.**36**

One of the results of this dirt and neglect was that a plague was spreading throughout the kingdom. King Augeas wanted to do something to prevent the plague. But the clean-up job was too

36 Oxters are armpits. Though, of course, cattle and sheep don't really have armpits. Let's say they were wallowing in dung up to their legpits.

big for anyone to undertake. And the undertakers
didn't want anyone to undertake the job because
the plague was good for business.

Eury came up with a bright idea. He set
Hercules the task of cleaning out King Augeas's
barns. But to make it doubly impossible, he said
that it had to be done in a single day.

"No worries," said Hercules. "No probs. No
drama."

When Hercules was within fifty kilometres of
the barns all he had to do was follow his nose.

He presented himself to Gorgeous Augeas that evening. Hercules told the king he would clean out his barns the next day. King Augeas laughed like a drain. (If you've never heard your drain laughing, I'm afraid you won't know what that sounded like.)

Augeas said, "Cleaning out my barns would take ten men ten years, and much longer unless we could persuade the animals to stop going to the toilet in the meantime. If you can do it in one day I'll give you half the fields that I own – and in my kingdom I own them all."

"Fair enough," said Hercules. "You're on."

First thing in the morning, Hercules knocked out the end walls of all the barns. Then he collected rocks and tree trunks and piled them on the bank of the nearby rushing river. When he'd got enough, he dug out a new watercourse. Then, with his rocks and tree trunks, he began building a dam across the river.

By mid afternoon he'd dammed the river and diverted the torrent so that it now surged along the new watercourse and through the barns. It rushed in at one end and out at the other. It rushed through one barn after another. Now, instead of being up to their oxters in smelly poo, the poor animals were up to their oxters in rushing water.

Still, no one could deny that the barns had been washed clean.

Hercules showed King Augeas what he had done. "Okay, King," he said, "which fields are mine?"

King Augeas looked worried for a moment. Then he smiled. "No fields for you," he said.

"Why not?" said Hercules.

"*You* didn't clean out the barns," said the king. "The river did."

"All right," said Hercules. "Tell the river to move the dam so that it can flow back along its proper course."

And with that, he stomped off home. "I hope your animals all get water on the knee, double pneumonia and leeches under their legpits," he muttered under his breath.

Each time Hercules came home from fulfilling one of his tasks, a mob of fans assembled outside the palace to cheer for him and to try to touch him or get an autograph, and a herd of sketching paparazzi[37] pursued him wherever

37 The paparazzi are people who chase after celebrities to take their picture. Nowadays the paparazzi take photographs which are quicker and easier to produce.

he went. And each time he came home, the crowd grew bigger.

Hercules was tickled pink,[38] but Eury didn't like it one bit.

"What, back already?" snarled Eury.

"Yep," said Hercules. "It was a breeze."

"A breeze?" said Eury. "I don't know what you're talking about. And get those paparazzi away from my palace."

"Easier said than done," said Hercules. "Is that my next task?"

"No," said Eury. "I've got something special planned for that."

"What is it?"

"It's a surprise," said Eury.

"Oh, goody," said the Big H. "I like surprises."

[38] Nobody actually tickled the Big H – nobody would dare to, nor did he turn pink. This is an old-fashioned expression that means he was very chuffed.

CHAPTER SEVEN

THE BIRDS OF THE STYMPHALIAN MARSH

For Hercules's next job, he found himself back in a bog. This time he was sent to kill a flock of people-pecking birds that were terrorising the region. Strange birds, they were. They were a mix between an eagle, a vulture and a crane (they could lift heavy weights), and their beaks, claws and wings were like brass.

You'd have thought the Big H would have been fed up with killing things by now – but a man's gotta do what a man's gotta do.

These people-peckers were doing quite a lot of killing themselves. And they had a novel[39] way of doing it. If they saw something that looked like a free lunch, they flew over in a flock.

39 This does not mean that they were bombing people with books. Novel, here, means new and unusual.

From their wings, they shed feathers that were like daggers. These rained down onto their prey. The prey could pray till the cows came home, and it wouldn't make any difference. Prayer was no shield against falling daggers, and the

people-peckers would just eat the cows as well. And it was no good trying to run away. The birds really enjoyed fast food. They would eat any creature they could get their sticky beaks into – they weren't fussy, although they were particularly partial to humans (especially chubby ones). Once the prey was cut to the quick[40] by the falling feathers, the flock would descend for the feast.

When they weren't carrying out bombing raids or enjoying the spoils[41] of their attacks, they nested in the spiky rushes that grew in the middle of the bog. And the bog was so soft and syrupy and slurpy that even Hercules couldn't wade through it.

He waited and waited for the flock to rise up so that he could shoot them out of the sky. But he waited in vain. (Which he was – vain, that is.) The birds had been gorging themselves silly. They were full to bursting, and all they wanted to do was to sleep in their nests. Then Hercules had a stroke of luck. Along came Athena, an old friend of his who was the goddess of odds and sods, including wisdom and war. She hated the marsh birds because they kept eating her pet owls. She happened to be carrying a huge rattle made of brass. Why Athena was wandering around a bog with a huge rattle made of brass, no one can explain. Anyway, Hercules asked if he could borrow the rattle and she was happy to lend it to him.

Hercules found a good spot on a rocky outcrop. He rattled his rattle like nobody's business. (Even when he was a baby he was the best at rattling a rattle.) The rattle made a deafening din that startled the birds so much that they all took wing.[42]

They squawked and screeched and whirled about in total panic. Hercules fired off arrow after arrow, hitting the birds in their soft underbellies. Two dozen birds fell dead or dying. When Hercules had run out of arrows he picked up a

[42] To take wing does not mean to take a wing, as you might at a roast chicken dinner, but to fly into the air.

large stone and hurled that. Over his head, one bird was flying above another. The stone killed them both stone dead. Hercules was the first person to kill two birds with one stone.[43]

[43] To kill two birds with one stone means to achieve two things at the same time.

Then, while he was running around reclaiming as many arrows as he could, Hercules suffered an aerial bombardment of falling daggers. But the blades could not penetrate the hide of Larry, the Lion of Doom, which Hercules wore on his back. Realising that their enemy could not be turned into a pin cushion, the rest of the squadron formed up, wheeled around (which is not easy when you haven't got any wheels) and flew off to search for a more peaceful bog elsewhere.

Hercules camped out beside the bog (despite the stench and the mosquitoes and the flies) in case the birds returned. He was so charming that Athena stayed with him. But by and by he became bored, and he returned home to tell his growing number of fans, and King Eury, that the birds had flown.

CHAPTER EIGHT
THE WHITE BULL OF CRETE

When King Eurystheus heard that Hercules had managed to get rid of the plague of people-pecking birds he was beside himself (which is a very hard place to be). He was running out of ideas. There must be some task he could set that would get the wretched man killed. If Hercules stayed alive, he might kill him and steal his kingdom. The people thought that Hercules was a hero, and they would be delighted to have the Big H as their king.

Then Eury received a message by sea mail. It was good news. King Minos, who ruled the faraway island of Crete, had a problem. A huge white bull that could breathe fire out of its nostrils had gone mad. It was running amok. It was ploughing up fields, knocking down walls, tearing up crops and goring to death any person that came within charging distance. It was charging like a wounded bull,[44] and it wouldn't accept cash or cheques. The people were too scared to venture out of the city to go to work. If the bull wasn't caught, they would all starve.

[44] To charge like a wounded bull means to charge too much for the work that was done.

That might do the trick, thought Eury. To Hercules he said, "I want you to nip over to my friend's island and fetch a white bull and bring him back here."

"I'm not a cowboy," protested Hercules. "I don't do cow-herding."

"He's not a cow," said Eury. "I told you, he's a bull."

"Haven't you got anything more difficult?" said Hercules. "Isn't there anything I can kill?"

"I'll think of something while you're away," said Eury."Just go and fetch the bull and stop arguing."

So Hercules went to Rent-a-Wreck, hired an old tub and sailed to the island. The city above the harbour had walls all around, and the great timber doors were locked and barred and barricaded. For an intercom, there was a little hole in the door. Hercules banged on the door. Soon a face

appeared at the hole. Hercules told the face he'd been sent to fetch a white bull, and asked where he could find it.

"It's a huge thing," said the face. "You can't miss it. It's out there somewhere. Help yourself. You're welcome to it."

"Right," said the Big H. "Boris, here I come!" He soon found the bull's tracks, and followed the trail of destruction. *I'm getting warm*, thought Hercules. (This was because it was midday in the middle of summer, and he was wearing a thick lion skin.) Then the ground

began to shake and shudder beneath his feet.

It must be an earthquake, he thought. Luckily, he glanced over his shoulder. Bearing down on him was the biggest bull he had ever seen. It was like a rhino in size and weight, but more like a racehorse in speed. Its red eyes were bulging, its black lips were frothing, its nostrils were shooting out fire like a flamethrower and its great feet were churning up a dust storm.

As it charged, the bull lowered its great head and turned it to one side. Hercules waited until

the point of the horn was about to pierce his
bellybutton. Then he did a quick sidestep (he was
the best at sidestepping). The bull's braking system
wasn't very efficient – as Boris careered past, Big
H leaped onto his back and seized the bull by the
horns.[45]

Boris skidded to a halt. He turned
around looking for Hercules, but
couldn't see him anywhere. *That's
funny*, he thought. *He was here a
minute ago.*

45 To seize the bull
by the horns means
to courageously and
decisively deal with a
dangerous or difficult
situation.

Hercules got a good grip on the horns, and wondered what he should do next. *I know*, he thought, *I'll twist and shout*. So he twisted and shouted. Boris crashed to the ground and Hercules rolled him onto his back. With his legs waving in the air, the bull was as helpless as a baby in a bassinet.**46** Boris rocked back and forth, but he couldn't roll over to get up again (rock'n'roll hadn't been invented back then). Hercules tied Boris's feet together. He fetched a bucket of water and put out

46 A bassinet is a wicker cradle with a hood – not to be confused with a basinet, which is a medieval helmet with a visor. Putting a baby in a helmet, or alternatively wearing a cradle on your head, is not to be recommended.

the fire in the bull's nose. Then he dragged Boris back to his boat.

As Hercules sailed away, the people realised what he had done. They rushed out of the city, ran down to the harbour and cheered their heads off. King Minos was happy to have got rid of the bull, but not happy about having lots of subjects without heads.

King Eurystheus wasn't happy either. Hercules dragged the bull into his chamber. In a flash, Eury was inside the urn again.

"What are you doing in there?" asked Hercules.

"What are *you* doing here?" asked Eury from inside the urn.

"You told me to fetch the bull," said Hercules. "So here it is."

"Just take it away," said Eury, shaking with fright.

"Make up your mind," said Hercules. "First you want it, then you don't."

So Hercules carted it off and released it on a plain outside the city, and it began to rampage around causing havoc, ploughing up fields, knocking down walls, tearing up crops and goring to death any person that came within charging distance. You can't blame it. A bull's gotta do what a bull's gotta do.

CHAPTER NINE

HORSES FOR COURSES

The next task involved another king and another kingdom. Kings were ten a drachma[47] in those days. Kings in general are a pretty unpleasant lot, but this king took the biscuit.[48] If there were no biscuits, he took the cake. If there was no cake, he threw a tantrum. He was mean and cruel in the extreme. His favourite game was waging war (not that he ever paid the troops their wages for waging). And his next favourite game was slaughtering peasants.

His name was King Diomedes, the ruler of Thrace, although Hercules called him King Diabolical. King Diomedes had

[47] Drachmas were the currency used in Greece until the introduction of the Euro. In ancient Greece, drachmas were coins made out of silver.

[48] Taking the biscuit means that this was the worst king of all. Imagine if you were having tea and your greedy great-aunt Jemima snatched the last chocolate biscuit and gobbled it up.

four horses. They had been reared to pull his war chariot. (It was rather alarming when they reared.) He fed his warhorses on nothing but human flesh.[49] Whenever he attacked and killed people, he let the horses feast on the corpses. When he was too busy doing nasty things to find time for a war, he invited guests for a sleepover at his palace. During the night, he would murder the visitors so that the horses could have a good breakfast.[50]

[49] As you know, normally horses are vegetarian and don't eat people. I am a vegetarian, and I don't eat people either.

Eury was sick and tired of Hercules. It seemed that whatever impossible task was set, Hercules managed to accomplish it – which just made the Big H more popular with the common people. And the common people didn't like Eury one bit. So Eury hatched a plan with King Diabolical. The correspondence was expensive in messengers. Every time Eury sent a message, Diabolical killed the messenger and fed him to the

[50] Even if you are not a horse, it's very important to start each day with a good breakfast. (I read that in a magazine.)

horses. But the plan was arrived at – and this was it: Hercules was told that Diabolical wanted him to tame the four savage horses and take them back to Eury as a gift.

"No worries," said Hercules. "No probs. No drama."

When Hercules arrived at Diabolical's kingdom, he would be told to get a good night's rest before starting his task the next morning. The evil king would murder Hercules during the night and feed him to the horses.

Eury would be happy: he would have got rid of Hercules for good. Diabolical would be happy: he would have been provided with a free meal for his horses. The horses would be happy: there was

plenty of meat on Hercules. Only Hercules wouldn't be happy – but then he wouldn't be unhappy either: he wouldn't know anything about it.

While Hercules was preparing for the journey, he bumped into his old mate Abderus, who was a horse tamer. Abderus said he'd like to go along for the ride (he enjoyed riding). Hercules asked Eury if that would be okay. "That's cool," said Eury, smiling. *More food for the horses*, he thought.

So Hercules and Abderus sailed off into the unknown. They were warmly welcomed by King Diabolical (who was sitting by the fire). He fed them

well (fattening them up), and showed them to their bedroom.

"I don't like the look of that Diabolical," said Abderus.

"Nor do I," said Hercules. "He kept looking us over as though he was weighing up how much meat we had on us."

"Do you think he's planning some dastardly deed?**51**" asked Abderus.

"I do," said Hercules. ("I do" is what you say when you are getting married. Hercules said "I do" even though he wasn't

51 A dastardly deed is an act that is mean, treacherous and cowardly.

getting married.) "But I don't intend to give him the opportunity."

Hercules and his friend didn't go to bed. Like shadows in the night, they slipped out of the palace and down to the stables, where they tied and gagged the grooms. (The grooms weren't getting married either). They found the horses chained to their mangers.**52**

52 A manger is a trough that animals eat their food out of. You can get more in a manger than you can on a plate.

"What will we do now?" asked Abderus.

"No problem," said Big H. With his sword, he whacked through the iron chains as though they were paper chains. Then they drove the horses before them and set off back to the ship.

You would have thought the noise made by the horses and their dragging chains would have been enough to wake the dead. But Diabolical had several dead lying around the palace and not one of them woke up. Diabolical woke though, and so did his guards. They rushed out in their nightshirts in hot pursuit (it was a warm night).

When Hercules reached his boat, he left Abderus to look after the horses while he hacked an opening in the seawall. The ocean rushed in and swept Diabolical and his guards off their feet, drowning them.

That was all very well. But hacking down seawalls takes time. When Hercules went back to the horses, he found them munching on a few bones, and no sign of Abderus anywhere.

"You haven't," said Hercules. "Have you?"

"Nay," said the horses.

But they smiled happily and licked their lips.

"Right," said Hercules, "what's sauce for the goose is sauce for the gander." (Why he said that, I'm not sure, as there was not a goose to be seen, nor a gander, and the horses had eaten Abderus without *any* sauce.)

In a rage, Hercules rushed back into the flood. He plunged in and floundered about until he found Diabolical, now nicely marinated.**53** He dragged the body out of the water and carried it back to the horses. By the time the horses had finished off

53 Marinated used to mean soaked in saltwater. Nowadays it refers to food that has been steeped in any liquid that might make it taste better.

Diabolical, they were so stuffed they could hardly move. Hercules took advantage of this and bound up their jaws. "Sorry, girls," he said, "but you're going on a diet – starting now."

Back home, he untied their jaws before he took them to see Eury. He thought Eury might want to check their teeth to see how old they were. But Eury didn't want to check their teeth. He didn't like the hungry look in their eyes. He preferred to sit in his urn, gnashing his own teeth, shouting instructions for them to be slaughtered.

CHAPTER TEN

THE GOLDEN BELT

King Eurystheus had a daughter named Admete. I don't know whether she was meaty or not, but I do know that she was a spoiled brat like most princesses. It was soon to be Admete's eighteenth birthday. She'd heard about a famous golden belt belonging to Hippolyte, Queen of the Amazons of Cappadocia.

"I want it!" she said.

"But it belongs to Queen Hippolyte, my little lemon blossom," whined Eury.

"Don't care," said Admete, stamping her foot. "Send your army to take it."

"But it's such a long sea journey, my little lily petal," whined Eury, "and the Amazon army is the most feared in the world. They've made mincemeat of every army that they've fought."

"Why?" asked Admete.

"I don't know," said Eury. "Maybe they like shepherd's pie."

"Well why don't they just catch a few shepherds to put in their shepherd's pie?" asked Admete.

"But they'd probably still want soldiers with

their boiled eggs," said her father.

"Well send that great hulk with the knobbly body and the smelly lion on his head," said Admete. "Everyone says he's invincible."

"Admete, my little grape pip," exclaimed

Eury in delight, "you're a genius, a chip off the old block. What a brilliant idea! Don't worry, my little rice pudding. Daddy will get his baby pussykins her golden belt."

Eury rubbed his hands together in glee.[54] If Hercules, by some miracle, brought back the golden belt, Eury would score some brownie points with his little diddums. But more likely the Amazons would skin Hercules alive and feed him to their dogs.[55]

Eury called Hercules and told him what his next task would be. Hercules didn't bat an eyelid.[56]

"No worries," said Hercules. "No probs. No drama."

Hercules organised a boat and a crew and set sail. It was an uneventful journey. Not a sign of a Cyclops[57] or the sound of a siren[58] the whole way.

When they put into port, Hercules sent a message to Queen Hippolyte (who Hercules laughingly referred to as Molly Muscles), inviting her to a candlelit dinner on board. There was

[54] Not to be confused with ghee, which is melted butter made from buffalo or cow milk. Eury rarely rubbed his hands together in that.

[55] The Amazons, incidentally, didn't live on the Amazon River. They lived in the north of Turkey. They were fearsome, frightening, fierce female warriors and no one had ever called one of them "my little dumpling" and lived till teatime.

[56] Batting an eyelid is something you should never do – it's very painful. But if you have to bat one, I recommend a vampire bat rather than a cricket bat.

[57] A Cyclops was a savage one-eyed giant.

[58] A siren was a wicked woman with a lovely voice who liked to shipwreck sailors.

always the chance that the messenger would be hanged, drawn and quartered by the first mob of Amazons he met – but Hercules was willing to take that risk.

Now, as a rule, Molly Muscles didn't like men. But Hercules was no ordinary man – any more than Molly was an ordinary woman. With her elite[59] guard standing by on the docks, she went on board. Hippolyte

59 The elite are the best of the bunch who have been selected and specially trained.

and Hercules were a perfect match. They went together as naturally as bubble and squeak.**60**

And Hercules was so charming that Queen Molly offered to give him a present.

"Why, thank you," said Hercules. "Please may I have your golden belt?"

"You may," she said. And she took it off and gave it to him.

At this moment, one of Queen Molly's bodyguards peeped through the porthole. She thought the handing over of the belt was a token of surrender, and she immediately raised the alarm. (The alarm had been lying on the deck.) "The incredible hulk is kidnapping our beloved queen!" she cried. "Attack!"

Suddenly, the romantic rendezvous**61** in the cabin was interrupted when Big H and Big M heard a racket on the deck (two of the sailors had been playing tennis). They rushed up to see what was going on. The first thing Molly Muscles saw was a sailor spearing one of her warriors, who was attempting to board the ship. Molly gave him a good belt (but not as good as her best golden one – she'd

60 When I was a kid, after the Second World War, bubble and squeak was what you ate on Mondays. You mixed together left over boiled cabbage and boiled potatoes and fried it in fat.

61 Rendezvous is a French word that means a get-together.

already given that one to Hercules) and knocked him into the middle of next week (around about 12 am on Thursday).

Hercules could see that his skeleton crew (sailors were very badly fed in those days) would soon be overwhelmed by the Amazon horde that was boarding the boat. Both he and Molly entered the fray. The battle continued until Molly lay dead at his feet.

Hercules ordered his mate (who was the mate) to put to sea. The Amazons who swam after the boat were speared like whales until they began to blubber. When the boat was far enough offshore to be safe from further attack, Queen Hippolyte was buried at sea.[62]

[62] To be buried at sea means to be wrapped in a flag and chucked overboard.

CHAPTER ELEVEN

THE GIANT KING OF TARTESSUS

King Eurystheus was dismayed that despite all of his scheming and plotting Hercules was still alive. The more tasks Big H completed, the more famous and popular he became. Eury wanted him out of the way. He racked his brains.[63] He barbecued his liver. He braised

---

[63] If you have any brains, I would avoid racking them at all costs.

his chops. The only idea he came up with during the meal was stealing the famous herd of cattle belonging to King Geryon of Tartessus. (Everyone had heard of this herd.) King Geryon lived a very long way away. Rustling his cattle would be no easy matter, and bringing them back would take ages. Besides, there was always the hope that King Geryon, who happened to be a giant and was a lot bigger even than the Big H, might stomp him. King Geryon was not someone you could easily mistake for anyone else – your dad, for example – not only because he was a giant, but because he had three bodies and heads and only one pair of legs. Just think of the problems he had to deal with. What would happen, for instance, if the three heads all wanted to go off in different directions at the same time? Or suppose that the first head wanted to do ballet, the second was determined to do kickboxing and the third was into Irish dancing! And believe me, even if all of him wanted to do what the rest of him wanted, he was not the sort of person you would want to meet up an alley on a dark night.

Hercules hated hanging around the palace seeing the spoiled brat, Admete, prancing around in Molly Muscles's belt, so he was quite pleased when he was given his next task. This time Eury refused to allow him a ship and crew, but Hercules was lucky enough to hitch a ride on a boat that was going in the right direction.

Eventually, when Hercules reached his destination, he was surprised to find that King Geryon's cattle were not black or white or brown, as you would expect, but red. Bright red. As red as tomato sauce. They were guarded by a cowboy called Eurytion and his four-footed friend, Orthrus. Orthrus was an interesting dog. He had two heads. Well, everyone knows that two heads are better than one.

"What's that rustling?" the cowboy said to his dog.

"It's only me shuffling through the leaves," said Hercules.

"Anyone who does any rustling around here is in for a surprise," said the cowboy.

"Oh, good," said Hercules. "I like surprises."

But then he got a surprise that he didn't like. Orthrus, baring two mouthfuls of fangs, leaped at the big fellow's throat. This presented a problem for Hercules because he didn't know which head to hit. He settled the matter by whacking them both. The cowboy had only one head – so Hercules whacked that as well.

King Geryon was not a pretty sight, but he had good hearing (he had six ears, so he had a head start on most people – a two-head start to be exact). King Geryon heard his herd. The cows were distressed about being herded by someone who wasn't their cowherd or his dog.

King Geryon came to see what was going on. Hercules hid behind a rock and waited until King Geryon drew level, he then fired one of his poison arrows. It went in one ear and out the other (like a reminder from your mother). It pierced all three brains. And King Geryon dropped down dead.

On the long journey home, Hercules found it difficult to keep the herd together. Various cows and bulls kept wandering off or stopping to graze or to have a snooze. He was forever running backwards and forwards, shouting, "Yee-hah!" at the top of his voice, and "Git along!" and other herding-like exclamations. He was getting a little hoarse.[64] He began wishing he'd brought a Big Horse. His dogs were killing him.[65] He wished he'd brought some dogs, as well.

One morning he awoke to discover that a thief had come in the night like a thief in the night and made off with two of the bulls. Hercules couldn't find a trace of them, but by and by he heard a low lowing (the bulls were lying down) coming from a cave.

Hercules confronted the thief in his lair. "I don't like people who steal cattle," said Hercules.

"*You* stole them," said the thief.

[64] Hercules was getting a sore throat, not from swallowing a horse like the old lady who began by swallowing a fly, but from all that yelling.

[65] Dogs is a slang word meaning feet. It is probably cockney rhyming slang. "Dog's meat" rhymes with feet. His dogs were killing him means that his feet were hurting. Well, I expect your feet would hurt if you'd walked as far as Hercules had.

LOW!

LOW!

"Why yes," said Hercules, scratching his head. "You've got a point there. I suppose I did."

"That means you don't like yourself," said the thief.

"I don't like you either," said Hercules.

The thief looked Hercules up and down. "I suppose you think you're big," he said.

"I *am* big," said Hercules.

"You're a wimp," said the thief. "I could tie you in knots."

"What sort of knots?" asked Hercules.

"Any sort," said the thief. "A reef knot. A granny. A clove hitch …"

"Go ahead," said Hercules. "Make my day!"

The thief tried a round turn with two half-hitches followed by a fisherman's bend.

But Hercules soon settled his hash.**66** (Hercules was the best at tying knots.) He left the thief coiled, kinked, snagged, snarled, spliced, tangled, twirled, twisted, tethered and tied, and went on his way.

66 To settle someone's hash means to subdue them in no uncertain manner.

The next day a swarm of horseflies descended upon the herd. The cattle began running about like headless chickens, some into the hills, some into the forest, some into the river. "Hey!" shouted Hercules to the horseflies. "They're cows, not horses!" But the flies went on biting the cattle anyway.

By then, the crimson cattle had run here, there and everywhere. It took Hercules more than a week to round them up. After months of hard slog, Big H got them back to Eury's palace. Hercules's fans went wild. The cheerleaders did a routine with red pompoms. The paparazzi had to sharpen their red colouring-in pencils. And a band played till the cows came home.

"Why are the cattle red?" asked Eury.

"Search me," said Hercules.

"Not while you're wearing that stinky lion skin," said Eury.

"Look at them," said Hercules. "Aren't they beautiful?"

"Yes," said Eury, his mouth watering. "Enough barbecued steak for a year!"

CHAPTER TWELVE

THE GOLDEN APPLES

By the time Hercules had returned home with the cattle, Eury had come up with a really difficult task – one he thought Hercules would have no chance of fulfilling.

"What's next?" asked Hercules.

"I want you to go and fetch three apples," said Eury, trying not to smirk.[67]

"Three apples?" said Hercules. "Easy-peasy."

[67] To smirk is to smile in a smug, conceited, silly way. Eury was the best at smirking.

"They're golden apples," said Eury, trying to keep a straight face. "And they only grow on one special tree."

"No worries," said Hercules.

"A ferocious dragon guards the tree," said Eury, trying not to laugh and nearly bursting. "He keeps his tail wrapped around the trunk and never sleeps."

"No probs," said Hercules.

"The garden where the tree grows is a very, very, very long way away," spluttered Eury. His face was as red as King Geryon's prize cows, and his eyes were bulging as if they were about to pop out.

"No drama," said Hercules.

"And one other thing," said Eury. "It's a *secret* garden. No one knows where it is." He couldn't contain himself any more. He laughed till he cried and fell on the floor clutching his stomach.

Afraid he might do something drastic that he'd regret later, Hercules picked Eury up

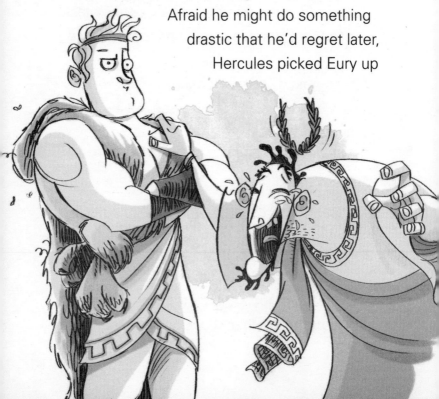

and stuffed him headfirst into the urn.

Big H travelled far and wide for many a long day – and many a short day, and lots of days of average length as well. He asked hundreds of people the same question: "Can you tell me where there's a secret garden with a special tree that grows golden apples and is guarded by a dragon?"

People thought he was out of *his* tree. "All brawn[68] and no brain," they said, and other non-complimentary things.

However, if at first you don't succeed, you should try and try again. Hercules was a sticker, as well as a stickler. No one could deny that. And finally, his persistence[69] paid off.

He was walking along a lonely beach one day, somewhere far from everywhere else, feeling fed up and cheesed off (he'd just been stuffing himself with bread and gorgonzola[70]), when he met three lovely sisters, and stopped for a chat. Hercules was at his most charming, and asked if they knew where the secret garden was to be found. They told him that the place he was looking for was the Garden of the Hesperides. They pretended that they didn't know where it was, but said they knew someone who did.

"Who?" demanded Hercules, not bothering to be charming any more.

"Our dad," he was told.

"Where is he?" demanded Hercules.

"You'll find him further along the beach – but he won't tell you," said one of the sisters.

We'll see about that, thought Hercules, and without so much as a "by your leave" a "thank you" or a "have a nice day", he charged off down the beach.

After a hundred-metre dash (Hercules was the best at hundred-metre dashes), Hercules caught sight of the old codger.[71] But when the old man saw Hercules approaching like an avalanche, he stood up and began to run towards the sea. Hercules made a diving tackle (he was the best at diving tackles) and got him in a half-Nelson (known in those days as a half-Samson). Hercules asked where the secret garden was. The old man wouldn't spill the beans (although he did spill his mutton and gravy – he was eating his lunch at the time). He just kept struggling, trying to get away. But Hercules wouldn't let him go. He

[71] An old codger is a mean or miserly or shabby old man.

began choking the old fellow. The old codger finally gave up the fight (and nearly gave up the ghost too).

"If I tell you," he gasped, "will you let me go?"

"I will," said Hercules.

So when the old man had recovered his breath and his wits, he gave precise directions.

"Thank you," said Hercules, being polite for a change.

"But it won't do you any good," said the old man.

"Why not?" asked Hercules.

"Because there's a dragon called Ladon that ..."

"No worries," said Hercules. "I know all about him."

"And anyone who picks the fruit will drop dead," said the old man, "except for a giant called Atlas. And he's busy."

"No probs. No drama," said Hercules. "I'll think of something."

And off he went, carefully following the old man's directions.

After many days of tiring travel, Hercules was getting warm. And there, in the mountains, just as the old codger had said, he came upon a giant. Hercules could see that this bloke would not be able to go and pick apples for him. The giant was chained to a boulder. To make matters worse for the poor chap, an eagle kept swooping out of the sky and pecking lumps out of him. The big fellow was using his hands to guard his eyes.

One poison arrow from our hero's bow, and the eagle swooped its last swoop and smacked into the ground! Then one mighty whack with his sword and the chain was split in twain. (They used to say twain in those days when they meant two.)

The giant peeped out from between his fingers.

"It's all right, Atlas," Hercules told him. "The eagle's dead. And you're free."

"Atlas?" said the giant, dropping his hands from his eyes. "Atlas? My name's not Atlas."

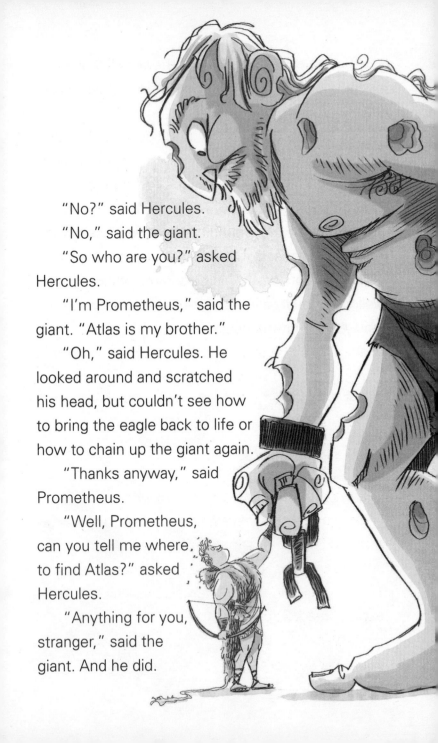

"No?" said Hercules.

"No," said the giant.

"So who are you?" asked Hercules.

"I'm Prometheus," said the giant. "Atlas is my brother."

"Oh," said Hercules. He looked around and scratched his head, but couldn't see how to bring the eagle back to life or how to chain up the giant again.

"Thanks anyway," said Prometheus.

"Well, Prometheus, can you tell me where to find Atlas?" asked Hercules.

"Anything for you, stranger," said the giant. And he did.

"I must have turned left at the last mountain instead of right," said Hercules. And off he went again.

But before Hercules found the giant, by chance he arrived in the valley containing the secret garden. And there, in all its glory, was the tree with the golden apples. And there, all gory, was Ladon the Dragon, laid on the ground. "No worries," said Hercules to himself. "No probs. No drama."

He fired off one of his poison arrows. Bullseye! Well, not literally a bull's eye – more a dragon's heart. Ladon bit the dust.

"I wouldn't bite the dust if I were you," said Hercules. "It's not good for the digestion." But that didn't matter because Ladon had expired. (He was past his use-by date.)

Hercules thought of helping himself to the apples there and then, but he was worried by what the old codger had said. He might drop dead on the spot.

Just then, he heard a groan. He looked up and caught sight of a figure near the top of the mountain. Hercules scrambled up (he was the best at scrambling).

A great tower of rock was tilted towards the valley below. A giant was straining to hold it up.

"Good day," said Hercules.

"It may be for you," said the giant. "There's nothing good about it as far as I'm concerned."

"What are you doing?" asked Hercules.

"What does it look like?" said the giant. "I'm holding up this rock."

"Why?" asked Hercules.

"I was told to," said the giant.

"Why?" asked Hercules.

"Because this rock is holding up the sky," said the giant.

Hmm, thought Hercules. *We've got a right one here.*

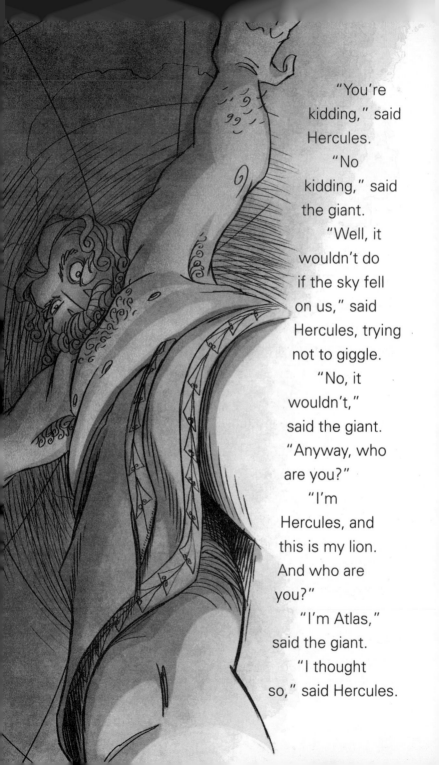

"You're kidding," said Hercules.

"No kidding," said the giant.

"Well, it wouldn't do if the sky fell on us," said Hercules, trying not to giggle.

"No, it wouldn't," said the giant. "Anyway, who are you?"

"I'm Hercules, and this is my lion. And who are you?"

"I'm Atlas," said the giant.

"I thought so," said Hercules.

"I've seen a book about you. I didn't actually read it – it was full of maps – but I saw your name on the cover."

"So what do you want?" asked Atlas.

"I'd like three of the golden apples off the tree below," Hercules said.

Atlas gave Hercules a thoughtful look. To have just a few moments relief from his burden would be more than wonderful. "You look like a strong fellow," he said. "I wouldn't do this for just anybody, but if you hold up this rock for me, I'll nip down and pick some apples."

I'd better humour him, thought Hercules. "All right," he said, "it's a deal."

Hercules didn't think that the tower of rock was actually holding up the sky, but the rock would certainly have come crashing down if no one was holding it up. He gradually took the weight from Atlas. "Not many people could do this," he said. "But I'm Hercules, champion of the world."

"Right," said Atlas. And he skipped off down the mountainside like a kid – that is to say, like a young goat. One moment he was overjoyed to be relieved of his burden. The next he was rather dismayed to find Ladon dead at the base of the tree. Still, he picked the apples and clambered back up again. "Some villain has killed my dragon," he said.

Hercules thought that it wouldn't be a good idea to admit to the crime. "Really?" he said. "I don't know what the world's coming to."

"The world will come to a nasty end if someone doesn't hold up the sky," said Atlas.

"You'd better get back here then," said Hercules.

But Atlas had enjoyed being free so much that he didn't want to take up the burden again. "What do you want these apples for?" he asked.

"I have to take them to King Eurystheus," Hercules said.

"Why don't you just carry on where you are? You're doing a great job. I'll take the apples to King Eurystheus for you. See you later, lion tamer."

Hercules realised that if Atlas went off with the apples he'd be left holding up the tower of rock forever. He still wasn't convinced that he was holding up the sky, but he didn't want to take the chance. One night in a storm a wet tent had fallen on him, and that was bad enough: he'd nearly suffocated under a couple of feet of wet canvas. If the whole sky came down, everybody would suffocate. It would be awful. And besides, if he let go of the rock it would crash down on top of him and he'd be splattered for sure.

"Good idea," he said. "I'm fed up with running errands for that twit. But before you go, can you just hold this up for a moment? It's pressing on a really sore spot on my shoulder. You take the weight and I'll fold up my lion skin to make a pad."

"Okay," said Atlas. "Be quick."

Atlas took the weight. Hercules slipped under his arm, grabbed up the golden apples and ran.

"Hey! Come back here," shouted Atlas.

But his shouts fell on deaf ears. A deaf old goatherd was watching his flock nearby, and

didn't hear a thing. Hercules heard all right, but ignored him.

"Don't drop the sky," Hercules called back, "or no one will ever be able to write a book about you again!"

The journey home was a lot quicker than the journey out. News that he was coming spread like wildfire before he arrived. This time the crowds were bigger than ever. The fans, the cheerleaders, the autograph hunters and the paparazzi surrounded him. He had to pose with the golden apples. The paparazzi didn't have gold colouring-in pencils, so they had to make-do with yellow. Although the Big H was a man of few words, the mob demanded he say a few words. "An apple a day keeps the doctor away," said Hercules.

Then he took the apples to Eury.

CHAPTER THIRTEEN

CERBERUS, THE HOUND OF HELL

The crowd outside the palace had been dazzled when Hercules let them see the golden apples, but King Eurystheus was not happy to see Hercules. He was pleased to see the golden apples though, and his greedy little eyes glinted.[72] He ordered a servant to take the apples away and have them locked in his treasury. But his immediate concern was what to do about Hercules. The next task, the twelfth, would be Herc's last. And Eury wanted to be sure that it was not only the last Hercules would undertake, but the last he would ever be able to undertake. If the Big H did return, Eury wanted to make sure that the only people happy to see him would be the undertakers.

[72] Not everyone's eyes can glint. Have a go in front of a mirror and see if yours can.

Eury gave the problem some thought. An undertaker is a person who takes someone under: under the ground. And this made Eury think about the Underworld. No one ever went down there and came back. He summoned Hercules into his presence. "You think you're so clever, don't you," he said to Hercules. "You think you can do anything."

"Well, whatever it is, I'll give it a go," said Hercules.

"All right then," said Eury, his face ugly with spitefulness. "Let's see you go down to the Underworld and bring back Cerberus, the Hound of Hell. I'd like to see that!"

"No worries," said Big H. "No probs. No drama."

The Underworld is a vast dungeon without sunlight or hope, where the dead suffer horribly and fade slowly and wretchedly into nothingness. Going down to the Underworld is not like going down to the Underground.[73] I mean, there aren't stations all over the place with signs to tell you where you are and adverts on the walls and buskers playing jolly tunes. And first you've got to find the entrance. That took awhile. But Hercules didn't give up. He wasn't a quitter. In the

[73] London's underground railway system, also known as the Tube.

end he found it in an isolated cave on a rocky shore *(so be careful the next time you go to the beach.)*

Cerberus belonged to King Hades and Queen Persephone, the king and queen of the Underworld. So Hercules thought it only proper to ask them if he could take their pet for walkies. When Hercules entered the cave, Cerberus appeared to be having a snooze – although with three eyes open. Cerberus was happy to let anyone go in. His job was to stop anyone getting *out*! The reason he snoozed with three eyes open was that he had three heads. He was the big brother of Orthus, the cattle dog, and much more scary. He had more teeth, for one thing. Three complete sets.

"Good dog, Fido," said Hercules as he passed. Cerberus curled three of his lips.

Hercules walked down the winding path that led into the bowels[74] of the Earth. The decomposing dead reached out their arms to touch him as he went by. He passed the Fate sisters, who held the thin threads of human life in their hands.[75] He passed the Fury sisters, who screamed their foul breath in his face, wanting to take vengeance on

[74] The bowels are the deepest or innermost part of something. For example, the bowels in your body are deep and innermost.

[75] There were three Fate sisters. One had power over every human's birth, one over their destiny and the third over their death.

newcomers for the wickedness of their lives.[76]

He came to the River Styx which was very wide
and murky, too wide and murky for
even the Big H to fancy a swim.
He approached a ferryman whose
name was Charon. Charon tried
to persuade him to turn back. But
Hercules insisted on being taken
across, and climbed into the boat.
Charon rowed laboriously[77] to the
other side. Hercules set off again
on foot, and eventually arrived at
the desolate palace of Hades and
Persephone.

[76] The Furies were
three ugly sisters who
worked for Hades and
Persephone, overseeing
the torture of people
who'd been naughty
or nasty and had
been consigned to the
Dungeons of the Damned.

[77] A laborious task is
one that takes a lot of
time and effort. Charon
couldn't complain:
Hercules's twelve
tasks were a lot more
laborious than rowing a
boat across a river.

"What the hell are you doing
here?" asked the king. "I didn't send for you."

"I just came to ask a favour," said Hercules.

"A favour!" spluttered the king. "You've got a
cheek!"

"Got two," said Hercules.

"He's cute," murmured the queen. "And brave.
And very *big*."

"He's all brawn and no brain," said the king.

"I just want to take Cerberus for walkies," said
Hercules. "I'll bring him back. Cross my heart and
hope to die."

"You'd better," said the king.

"I'd better what?" asked Hercules.

"All three," said the king. "In any case, you can try, but I don't think he'll go with you."

So Big H went back to the river. "You look as happy as a dog with two tails," said the ferryman, as he rowed him across.

He must mean like a lion with two tails, thought Hercules. He tried to look behind his back – but he could only see one.

Hercules made his way past all the scary creatures who screeched and moaned and touched him with their dead fingers. And finally he came face to face with Cerberus.

"Hello again, Fido," said Hercules. Now, all of Cerberus's six eyes were open. As you know, anyone could pass in, but no one ever passed out. (Other than fainting from fear.)

Cerberus was not a lap dog. Cerberus was not a common or garden pooch. Cerberus was a ripper. With three heads. Cerberus was as big as a lion. Poison dripped from his fangs. He snarled. Hercules snarled back.

Cerberus was a bit put out (dogs are often put out – especially if they pee on the carpet). With his lion head on top of his own, Hercules looked like a small giant with two heads. *That's all right*, thought Cerberus, *it's still three against two in my favour*.

They circled each other for awhile and squared up (Hercules was the best at geometry). Then suddenly Cerberus sprang. But Hercules was ready. He whipped off his lion skin (which smelled like an old dog), hurled it over the three heads of the smelly old dog, wrapped it tight and tied it around with his lion's tail. *That's another job nicely wrapped up*, thought Hercules. (Hercules was the best at dogfights.)

But the fight wasn't over yet. Cerberus didn't give up that easily. He struggled and squirmed for half an hour, trying to get a head free, or trying just to get ahead, but to no avail. He couldn't breathe.

He felt as though the sky had fallen on him. And all the time, Hercules held the dog in an iron grip and squeezed as though Cerberus was a giant lemon ready for juicing.

Then, with a despairing whimper, Cerberus ceased struggling and lay still.

"Good dog, Fido," said Hercules. "Stay! I've got something for you: three bones." As he'd passed the rotting deceased, Hercules had collected three fresh-looking bones with plenty of meat – one for each head.

Bones! thought Cerberus. *Why didn't you say?* If Cerberus had known he was going to get bones, he wouldn't have been so difficult in the first place.

Hercules unwound the lion skin from the hound. He gave Fido the bones. Cerberus immediately dug three holes and buried the bones in a row.

"Now we're going to go walkies," said Hercules.

When Cerberus heard the magic word, "walkies", he leaped and pranced with delight, and nearly wagged his tail right off. Nobody had taken him for a walk in years. *Why didn't he say before, the great twit?* thought Cerberus. *He must be all brawn and no brain.*

So Cerberus dogged his new master's footsteps all the way to King Eury's palace. A multitude lined the road and cheered. Hercules, with Cerberus at heel, marched into Eury's chamber. Eury began to quake in his sandals,[78] and then leaped into his urn. Cerberus looked at the urn suspiciously and slavered and growled. He walked all around it, sniffing. Then cocked his leg.

[78] This is not easy to do. If you have any sandals, try quaking in them and you'll see what I mean.

"Get that thing out of here!" cried Eury. His quaking made the urn quiver. "Put it back where it came from. And get out of my sight. I never want to see you again!"

"Well!" Hercules said to Cerberus. "I've been his dogsbody[79] – if you'll pardon the expression – for ten years. And that's all the thanks I get."

[79] A dogsbody is someone who is given all the boring and menial jobs. Cerberus, of course, had a dog's body of his own.

CHAPTER FOURTEEN
FAMOUS LAST WORDS

Hercules wandered the world with no fixed abode, but his fame went before him, as did his shadow when the sun was on his back. He was welcomed in many castles and palaces where they had some jobs for him to do.

He met a princess whose name was Deianeira. He was old, but still charming, so they got married.

One day Hercules and Deianeira were out walking when they came to a river in flood. Hercules could swim across, of course, but Deianeira was frightened of the strong current.

Hercules said, "Just hold onto my shoulders."

Deianeira said, "No way. I'm not going to hug that smelly old lion skin. You've got to be joking."

While they were arguing, along came a centaur named Nessus. (A centaur had the body of a horse and the head and shoulders of a man – which I think you'll agree is a pretty kettle of fish.)[80]

"I'll take her across," Nessus said. "She can ride on my back."

"Good man," said Hercules. "That is to say, good horse … er … I mean, good for you."

[80] A pretty kettle of fish is a saying that means a muddle. It is an old-fashioned phrase, but I like it. I have a pretty kettle, as a matter of fact, but I don't keep fish in it.

"I'll race you to the other side," said Nessus. "Ready, steady, go!"

Hercules could never refuse a challenge. He wanted to be the best at everything. He ran to the river, plunged in and swam to the far bank. "I won, I won!" he yelled. But then he looked back and saw that Nessus had tricked him. Nessus was galloping off with Deianeira on his back. Hercules drew his bow and fired off one of his poison arrows. Nessus stumbled and fell dying in the dust.

"I'm sorry, Deianeira," Nessus whispered. (He whispered because he wasn't half hoarse – even though he was half-horse.) "It was wrong of me. To make amends, take some blood from my wound. If you smear my blood on Hercules he will never love anyone but you."

And with that, he kicked the bucket (which happened to be lying nearby).

So when Hercules was asleep, Deianeira

smeared him with the centaur's blood. But it didn't have the effect she expected. Nessus had deceived her. Poison from the Hydra – the poison Hercules had used to kill Nessus – was mixed with Nessus's blood. When Hercules tried to rise, he collapsed and appeared to be knocking on death's door.

Deianeira, in wanting him to love her, had brought about this disaster. Hercules's charming days were over. Deianeira lay down on their bed and stabbed herself in the heart out of grief.

With his wife dead, and himself in so much pain, Hercules gave orders for a pyre[81] to be built. When it was ready, his men laid him upon it. His club was his pillow. His lion skin was his blanket. Then he played the lyre for the last time, and in a faint voice told his friends to light the fire.

81 A pyre is a bonfire for a funeral ceremony.

"Do you think it's a good idea for you to start smoking at your age?" said the bearer of the flaming torch.

"No worries," said Hercules. "No probs. No drama."

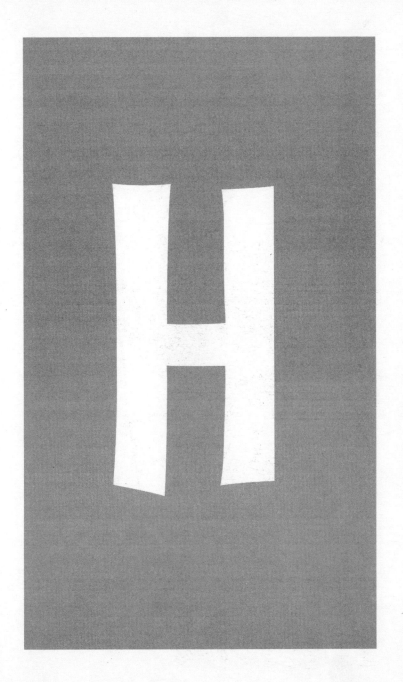